# Max's Amazing Models

For my mum and dad, who helped me go to university
to become an illustrator.

C.J.

# EGMONT
*We bring stories to life*

## Book Band: Orange

First published in Great Britain 2016
This Reading Ladder edition published 2016
by Egmont UK Limited
The Yellow Building, 1 Nicholas Road, London W11 4AN
Text copyright © 2016 Linda Chapman
Illustrations copyright © Chris Jevons
ISBN 978 1 4052 7823 2
www.egmont.co.uk
A CIP catalogue record for this title is available from the British Library.
Printed in Singapore
60879/1

**Series and book banding consultant: Nikki Gamble**

MIX
Paper
FSC  FSC® C018306

# Max's Amazing Models

Linda Chapman
Illustrated by Chris Jevons

**Reading Ladder**

Max likes making models. He makes his models out of card, plastic and glue, and anything else he can find!

Monster Shampoo!

ashing Liquid

Model Making

But Max's models aren't ordinary
models. Max has a magic power button –
and it makes all his models come to life!

Max often needs his models to help
him. Like the time a monster invaded
his bedroom.

The monster made a big mess. It threw all of Max's toys around and put Max's clothes on the floor and even knocked over some of his models. Then the monster hid inside the wardrobe.

Max needed to make a model
to help him stop the monster.

What should
I make?

A boat? A motorbike? No. An alien with

six arms of course!

Soon the alien was ready. Max pressed
the magic power button.

The alien came to life!

Max opened the wardrobe door and

the alien ran inside.

BUMP! CRASH!

The monster was big but it couldn't fight off six arms. The alien tickled the monster so hard that the monster gave up and ran away.

The alien helped Max tidy up.

After that, the messy monster never invaded his room again.

The next morning Max packed his bag
for school.

15

On his way to school something very strange happened.

A wheelie bin started to follow him.

17

The lid of the wheelie bin opened wide.

It had pointy teeth and a slimy tongue.

The wheelie bin came closer. It looked hungry. Max ran.

Max didn't stop until he was safe inside
the classroom.

Max was worried about the wheelie bin. What if it tried to eat someone?

Max needed to make a model to help stop the wheelie bin.

A red spaceship with rocket blasters
of course!

The wheelie bin was waiting for Max at playtime. It licked its lips and started to move closer.

Max pressed the magic power switch.
The spaceship came to life. It flew up
into the air.

WHOOSH! The spaceship blasted
soapy water right inside the bin. There
were bubbles everywhere.

28

The bin shrieked and gurgled. It did
not like soap. Its lid slammed shut.

After that the playground was much cleaner. And the evil wheelie bin never tried to eat Max again.

31

At the weekend, Max was invited to
Josie's Pirate Party.

Max took his model-making kit with him just in case.

The children left Josie's presents in the kitchen. Her pirate cake looked delicious!

After you've played outside. There are lots of balls in the garden.

Can we have some cake?

Max was in the garden when he saw three ninja sheep.

Birthday Baaandits!

Max needed a model to stop the ninja sheep.

Max made a robot that could shoot
plastic balls from its tummy.

But the sheep had already found the presents. The robot needed to get there fast.

Max stuck pirate eye patches on to the robot to make wings.

Max pressed the magic power button.

Now!

The robot flew at the sheep.

# POW! POW!

Plastic balls flew up into the air.

The sheep liked the balls and ran to pick them up.

The other children cheered. They grabbed more balls and threw them down the garden.

The sheep forgot all about the cake and the presents and chased after the balls.

Max, his robot and the other children had all saved the party together!

And the ninja sheep never stole birthday cake again.

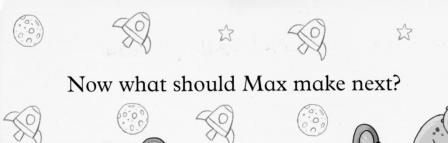

# Now what should Max make next?